SALLY NICHOLLS
A Lily, A Rose

To all the many people who play games
with me. You know who you are.
Thank you.

LONDON BOROUGH OF WANDSWORTH	
9030 00003 3553 6	
Askews & Holts	25-Apr-2013
JF TEENAGE 11-14	£6.99
	WWX0010837/0123

First published in 2013 in Great Britain by
Barrington Stoke Ltd
18 Walker Street, Edinburgh, EH3 7LP

www.barringtonstoke.co.uk

ISBN: 978-1-78112-196-2

Printed in China by Leo

Contents

Chapter 1
Friends

When I was fourteen, my cousin Dan was my favourite person in the whole world.

Dan came to my father's castle when I was thirteen. He was going to be a knight when he grew up, and his parents sent him to live with us so that he could learn about fighting from Father.

Father was a knight. He'd been in lots of battles in Scotland, against Robert the Bruce and the Scots. When I was little, he was away for years, fighting in the war and living in the King's palace in Westminster. But when the new king, King Edward was crowned, Father came back home. I knew why. Father was a friend of Roger Mortimer, the man who killed King Edward's father. And Roger Mortimer and his friends weren't very popular in Westminster when King Edward took the throne.

Father minded not being in Westminster, but I liked it. I liked having him home. Mother died when I was small, so I used to get very lonely when Father was away at war.

And then Dan came. I was so excited. I didn't know many people my own age, only the younger servants, and some of the soldiers who guarded the castle. I didn't have any brothers or sisters. There weren't any families near to us with children. Before Dan came, my best friends were my maid, Alice, and my horse, Moonlight. I loved Alice and Moonlight, but horses can't talk, and Alice was very bossy. She was always telling me off for talking too much, or getting mud on my new dress, or running across the yard shouting. She wanted me to act like a lady.

I was a lady. Lady Elinor of Hardford Castle. I didn't feel like one. Most of the time, I felt like a little girl.

Fourteen wasn't old enough to be a lady yet.

When Dan came, I was so happy. We did everything together. We went riding, and hunting. We played dice and chess in the evenings. We read books out loud and giggled at the rude bits. It was lovely to have a friend the same age as me. Dan liked to be silly, just like I did. We used to pull faces at each other in church, and see who could make the other one laugh first. We swam in the castle moat. We spent whole afternoons eating plums and apples from the orchard. It was wonderful.

One evening, we were all in the parlour. Our parlour was a small, warm room, with wooden panels round the walls and pictures of knights and ladies, woven in wool.

The fire was burning in the middle of the room. My maid, Alice, was mending a new hole in my dress. Father was writing at his table in the corner.

Dan and I were playing chess. I loved chess. It was my best, best thing. I could play it all day long and be happy.

Dan preferred dice, or backgammon.

"I don't see why we always play chess," he grumbled. "You *always* win."

"That's because I'm better than you are," I told him. "I'm better than you at everything! I'm better at riding – and hunting – and dancing – "

"Elinor," said Alice. "Behave yourself. Ladies don't boast."

I stuck out my tongue. Dan giggled.

"I'll always be better than you," I told him. "You'll never beat me!"

"Want to bet?" he asked.

"Bet what?" I said. "That I'll always be better at everything?"

"No," said Dan, "that you'll win this game of chess."

Had he gone mad? Dan might be better than me at – oh, shooting arrows, and fighting with swords and other boy things. But I was always, always better at chess.

"Let's bet," said Dan. "If I win, you have to give me something. And if you win, I'll give something to you."

"Like what?" I asked. It sounded like a trick to me. Dan would maybe give me a kick, or a handful of mud, or a dead toad.

"Something nice," said Dan. "The loser can choose what they give. But it has to be something good."

It seemed like an odd bet, but it sounded interesting.

"All right," I said.

That evening, Dan played *really* badly.

"Are you *trying* to lose?" I asked.

"No!" Dan said. But he lost anyway.

"I won!" I shouted. "I won! What do I get? What do I get?"

But Dan wouldn't tell me.

"Not here," he said. "It's a secret. I'll give it to you tomorrow, after lessons."

Every morning I had lessons with our priest, Father Henry. I learned Latin, and Greek, and English, and all about God and Jesus. Dan learned knight things, like shooting and fighting with a sword and jousting with Father. Dan couldn't even say 'hello' in English.

"Why should I learn English?" he said. "Everyone important speaks French."

It was true. But Father told me that a lady should know English as well.

"One day you'll have your own house and your own servants," he said. "And you should know how to speak to the people who work for you."

After lessons, I went to the yard to watch Dan shoot arrows. The yard was a big open space inside the castle walls. It was always full of noise and people. Three grooms were exercising horses, riding them round and round in a circle. A little boy was feeding the chickens by the kitchen door. Two of Father's soldiers were playing with a dog. And Father was watching Dan shoot arrows at a target.

Dan put down his bow as soon as he saw me.

"Are we done, sir?" he asked Father.

Father smiled. "All right," he said. "I'll see you at dinner."

I went with Dan to help put the bows and arrows away.

"Where's my present, then?" I said. "Is it ready?"

"It's ready," said Dan. Suddenly, he looked nervous. "Close your eyes."

I closed my eyes and held out my hands. But Dan didn't put anything in them.

He kissed me, on the cheek.

Chapter 2
Secrets

I was so surprised. I opened my eyes and stared at him.

"What did you do that for?" I asked.

"Because ..." said Dan. He looked shy. "Because I love you."

"You *love* me?" I said.

"Yes. I do."

I was amazed. Dan loved me! How wonderful!

"Did you like it?" he said. "Being kissed?"

"Well ..." I felt myself go red. "Well, yes. I did like it."

"Good," said Dan. He kissed me again.

And that's how Dan and I fell in love.

I loved being in love with Dan. It was my secret, a secret only Dan and I – and Alice – knew.

I thought about Dan all the time. I'd be working, or eating, or sewing, and I'd think 'I'm in love with Dan' and my whole body would start smiling. I'd be talking to Father, and I'd think, 'I'm in love with Dan! And he's in love with me!' and I'd start laughing for no reason at all.

When I wasn't with him, I'd close my eyes and imagine I was holding his hand, or kissing him, or telling him secrets, and I'd feel so happy.

No one else knew. I thought people would guess, just by looking at us. But no one ever did.

My maid Alice was the only person I told. I couldn't keep a secret from Alice. After lessons, we sat in the parlour by the fire and sewed and talked about love.

Alice was in love with Red-Haired Harry, who was the head cook.

"He blew me a kiss last night," she said. "He *is* lovely!"

"Are you going to marry him?" I asked, but Alice laughed.

"Not me!" she said. "I don't want a house, and lots of babies. I just want a bit of fun while I'm young." She looked at me, sly. "I want a nice young man to keep me warm at night. That's all."

"Alice!" I said. I was shocked. "You don't mean you and Harry would ... do *that*, do you? Before you're married?"

"Why shouldn't we?" asked Alice. "If you can't have a bit of fun, what's the point of being alive?"

I was quiet. I didn't like to think about Alice being sinful.

"Don't you mind about going to hell?" I said.

"I know I should," said Alice. "But I've done it now. And God only forgives your sins if you're truly sorry, and I'm not. I try to be, but I'm not.

Why should I be sorry about a bit of fun? So if I'm going to hell anyway, I might as well enjoy myself now."

"But what if you had a baby?" I said.

"Oh, well ..." she said. "Then I'd have to marry Harry, wouldn't I? He'd look after me. I'd be all right."

I sat and sewed in silence for a bit, thinking.

"So," said Alice. "Tell me about you and your Dan."

"Oh ..." I said. "He's lovely too ..."

"And you two don't – " Alice asked.

"Of course not!" I said, shocked. "Dan's a gentleman. He'd never do anything like that."

"Hmm," said Alice.

After dinner, I went riding with Dan. I rode Moonlight fast up the road from the castle. Dan galloped behind me.

"Wait for me!" he shouted, but I didn't. I galloped as fast as I could. At the top of the hill, I stopped and waited for him to catch up.

"You're mad!" shouted Dan. "I love you, but you're ridiculous!" I laughed. I was mad, and Dan loved me, and I was so happy.

We had a good ride. We rode through the forest and back home over Father's fields. It was cold and the sky was a pale white-blue. The sun was setting behind us.

"Will you love me forever?" Dan asked.

"I don't know," I said. I loved teasing him. "Will I love you when you're fat and grey and old?"

"I'll love *you* when you're fat and grey and old," said Dan. "I'll love *you* when you're half-blind, with no teeth."

"Yuck!" I said. "If your teeth fall out, I'll ditch you and get someone better."

"You wouldn't really," said Dan. "Would you?" But I just laughed.

In the stable, we brushed the horses down together.

"*I'll* love you forever," said Dan. "*I* can't imagine not loving you."

I thought for a moment.

"I can't imagine not loving you either," I said.

Dan smiled. He looked so sweet and happy that I leant forwards and kissed him, on the mouth.

Dan blinked. But then he kissed me back.

We kissed. And kissed.

"I'm sorry," he said, when we pulled apart. "I didn't mean ..."

"I don't mind," I said. "I liked it."

I leant towards him. Our lips touched.

The door opened behind us.

It was Father.

Chapter 3
Angry

Father stood in the stable doorway, glaring at me and Dan. Then he marched over and grabbed my arm.

"What are you doing?" I said. "Let me go!"

"Come with me," said Father. "Right now."

I'd never seen him look so angry before.

He dragged me out of the stable and across the yard. The soldiers working on their shooting stopped and stared at us. Father pulled open the wooden door at the North Tower and pushed me up the stairs and into his room.

Father's room was small and busy. The walls were oak panels and there were tables for Father, his steward, and the other men who work in the castle. Father's table was covered in piles of parchment, ink-horns, quills and wax. He shut the door behind us and turned to face me.

"How long has this been going on?" he demanded. His voice was low and angry.

"That's private," I said. "It's nothing to do with you!"

Father's face was purple.

"It has *everything* to do with me," he shouted. "I'm your *father*. Do you know what would happen to you, if people found out you'd been kissing Dan in stables? Who do you think would want to marry you then?"

"I don't care!" I said. "I wouldn't want to marry them either! I want to marry Dan!"

"Ha!" said Father. "Well, let's be clear on one thing, my girl. Dan's father will never let him marry you. Dan needs to marry a girl with money – you know that. And you need to marry a man with connections to the King."

I was so angry, I was nearly crying.

"I don't care what you want," I shouted. "We'll run away together and get married and you can't stop us!"

"If you do," said Father, "I will put you in a nunnery and never speak to you again."

We glared at each other. I hated him. I hated him. I wanted to throw him on the rubbish-heap. I wanted the castle to fall down on his head and kill him. I wanted ravens to peck his eyes out, and dogs to eat his bones.

"You are not to speak to Dan again," said Father. "You are not to go out riding with him. When you're not in lessons, or at meals, you are to have Alice with you at all times. I'll tell her."

"But – " I said.

"Be quiet!" Father shouted. "I'm going to write to Dan's father and tell him that Dan is to go back home. Tomorrow."

"But you can't – " Now I was really frightened. "Please, Father," I said. "Please. I'll do anything you say. Please let Dan stay here – "

"No!" Father shouted. And don't think this is over with you yet."

I turned and ran out of the r What would I do if Dan went away. ever be happy again?

The next two weeks were horrible.

Father was so angry. He stamped aroun. the castle shouting at the servants. Dan and I weren't allowed to be alone together, ever. Everywhere I went, Alice had to come too. She came riding with me. She took me to and from lessons. She sat next to me in church. Dan had to stay in the yard, working on his shooting and fighting. I had to stay upstairs doing my lessons. Latin. English. Sewing. Weaving. Singing and playing the harp.

The only good thing was that Father didn't send Dan away. If he had, Dan's father would have asked why, and Father didn't want anyone know about me and Dan. He was trying to find somewhere else for Dan to live. He kept sending out messengers with letters.

time I saw Dan, he looked unhappy. sat together at dinner, he was almost . I wanted to talk to him, but I couldn't ut how. Not with Alice watching.

lice and I fought every day.

"I need to see Dan," I said.

"No, Elinor." Alice shook her head.

"But why *not*? You could watch us. We wouldn't do anything."

"Elinor, I can't," said Alice. "I promised your father."

"Well, can't you give him a letter from me?" I asked. "You could read it first."

"Elinor, no." Alice was firm. "Your father would be so angry if he found out. He'd send me away. I'd lose my job."

"If you don't let me see Dan," I said, "I'll tell Father about you and Red-Haired Harry. Then you will lose your job."

Alice shrugged.

"I thought I could trust you," she said. "But if you want to betray me, I can't stop you."

I clenched my fists. Of course I'd never betray Alice. She and Dan were the best friends I had in the world.

"Aargh!" I kicked the bedpost. The bed shuddered. "Please, Alice. Please, please, please, please, *please*. I just want to talk to him. That's all."

"I'm sorry, Elinor." Alice did look sorry. "The answer's no."

"I hate you!" I shouted.

There was a knock at the door.

It was one of Father's servants.

"Lady Elinor," he said. "Your father wants to see you. He has some news for you."

Chapter 4
A Plan

Father was in his room, writing. No one else was there. He looked up as I opened the door.

"Elinor," he said. "My darling. How are you?"

For the first time in weeks, he didn't sound angry. He sounded gentle. Almost happy.

I went stiff. How dare he be gentle?

"I'm still here," I said, stiffly.

"Good," said Father. He didn't seem to notice that I was scowling at him. "You're growing into a lovely young woman, Elinor."

This was all very strange. Why wasn't he angry any more?

"It must be dull for you," said Father. "Living here, with no other girls your own age."

"I don't mind," I said. "I like living here."

"Still ..." Father said. "You're growing up."

There was a pause. I waited. 'Please, Father,' I thought. 'Whatever it is, tell me.'

Father took a deep breath.

"I have some news for you, Elinor," he said. "You're going to be married."

Married! Me, married!

"Who to?" I asked.

"His name is Sir William of Courtney," said Father. "We fought together in Scotland. He's a good man."

I swallowed. I felt like I was going to cry.

"How old is he?" I asked.

"How old?" Father looked surprised. "About as old as I am. He's got a grown-up son, and a daughter your age."

"And – is he handsome?"

"Handsome!" Father laughed. "What do you think? He's a grown man, Elinor. He's got grey hair and a beard and a limp. He's a good man. That's what's important."

He was laughing at me. 'Silly little Elinor, wanting a handsome husband.' That's what he was thinking.

I didn't know what to think. I didn't know what to say. I always knew Father would find me a husband, one day. But not yet! Not so soon!

How could I marry an old man, Father's age?

How could I share an old man's bed?

How could I marry anyone, when I loved Dan so much?

"I won't do it," I said.

"What did you say?"

"I won't do it," I said, again. "I won't. I *can't*. I'm in love with Dan."

Father's face went pink.

"Enough of this nonsense!" he said. "You and Dan will *not* be married. His father wouldn't allow it, and neither would I."

I wanted to push him into the fire.

"If you make me do this," I said. "I will pay you back. I'll be so horrible to Sir William that he won't ever want to marry me. I'll pull his beard and spit in his face and tip his soup up over his head. I'll make love to his servants. I'll tell him about Dan. He'll think I'm *crazy*."

Father's face went as red as a ripe plum.

"Sir William is coming here on Monday to meet you," he said, his voice low. "If you so much as *frown* at him, I'll send Dan back to his father, and you'll never see him again. I'll feed your horse to the hounds. I'll cut off your hair and turn it into a *rug*. I mean it, Elinor."

"Please," I said. "Please, please, Father, don't make me get married. Not to an old man. I'm too young. I'm only fourteen. Let me stay here, just for a little bit longer. Please!"

"Stay here?" said Father. "After how you and Dan behaved? Do you think I'm a madman?"

I looked at the floor.

"I'm sorry," I said. "I'm so sorry, Father, please. I didn't mean it."

Father sighed.

"I'm not trying to hurt you," he said. "I'm trying to look after you. This new king doesn't like our family very much, and we need all the friends we can get. Sir William will take care of you. And I don't think you and Dan should live together any more."

I knew what he meant, and I felt myself go red. Dan and I wouldn't do *that*.

Would we?

No, of course we wouldn't.

But the longer I knew him, the more I loved him.

And the more I loved him, the more I wanted to kiss him, to touch him, to show him how much I liked him.

Maybe it was a good idea to keep us apart.

If we couldn't be married, maybe it was better not to see him.

No! No, it wasn't!

If I couldn't be with Dan, I'd never be happy.

Never, never, never, never, never!

I'd just have to think of a plan.

A plan to stop Sir William of Courtney marrying me.

A plan that would let me marry Dan.

I could do it.

I had to.

Chapter 5
Love

Alice was in our room, weaving a new bolt of cloth. Father's servant took me to the door, and watched me go in. I waited until he'd gone, then I said.

"Father wants me to be married!"

"*Married?*" Alice stared. "Who to?"

"To some horrible old man," I said. "Can you imagine anything *worse*? I don't want to get married to an old man! I'd die! I know I would!"

"What are you going to do?" Alice asked. She looked serious.

"I don't know!" I said. "But I *can't* marry him, Alice. I just *can't*."

"Maybe you could be a nun instead," Alice said.

"A *nun!*" I pulled a face. "Alice, no! I don't want to be a *nun*. I want to marry Dan."

"Did you tell your father that?" Alice asked.

I nodded. "It's no good. He won't let us." I squeezed my hands tight together. "Maybe we should run away. We could live in a house in the woods somewhere. We could grow things, and hunt for food. You could come, Alice!"

"No, I couldn't," said Alice firmly. "And if you go, I'll tell your father. A young lady like you – living like a beggar!"

"I wouldn't mind," I said.

"Well, I would," said Alice. "And so would your father. He'd bring you straight back home. And imagine what would happen if you spent a night in the woods with Dan! Nobody would ever marry you. You really would have to be a nun then."

"Aargh!" I fell back onto the bed. "What shall I *do*, Alice?"

"I think you should meet this man," said Alice. "Don't look like that! If he's awful, then tell your father you won't marry him. But maybe you'll like him."

"I'll never like him," I said. "Never. *Never*."

"Your father loves you," Alice said. "He'll have chosen a good man. You should meet him."

"I don't want to marry Sir William!" I shouted. "I want to marry Dan! I wish I was a boy. Then I could do whatever I wanted!"

But Dan was a boy, and he couldn't do whatever he wanted either.

After a while, I went to the stables to see Moonlight. Alice came and waited by the door. I gave Moonlight an apple, and she licked my fingers to say 'thank you'.

"What am I going to do, Moonlight?" I said.

Moonlight blew warm air onto my fingers. 'I love you.' That's what she was saying.

Alice was right. Father loved me too. He'd be furious if I said no to this Sir William before I even met him.

But he wouldn't force me to marry someone I hated.

I knew what I was going to do. I would meet Sir William and then I'd tell Father that I hated him. And then Father wouldn't make us get married.

"And I will hate him," I told Moonlight. "I'll never love him. Never, never, never, never, never!"

Chapter 6

A Lover

In the days before Sir William came, I did lessons in the mornings and in the afternoons. I had to practice my sewing, and my harp and my singing. I hoped Sir William liked music. Maybe my dreadful singing would put him off wanting to marry me.

Nobody made me work on any of the things I was actually good at, like chess, or riding, or hunting. Nobody cared that I could ride faster than Father, or train a falcon. I just had to know how to read Latin, and speak English to the servants, and sew a tablecloth.

On Monday, at breakfast, Father said, "Elinor, Sir William is coming here this evening. He'll stay with us for two nights, so you can meet each other."

I swallowed and looked down. My heart began to beat faster.

"Why do I have to meet him?" I asked. "I know I'm going to hate him. I *know* it."

"Elinor," said Father. He gave a big sigh. "He's a good man, I swear it. I wouldn't let you marry a bad one."

"Would you let me marry a man I hated?" I asked.

Father was quiet.

"No," he said. "If I really, truly thought you hated Sir William, I wouldn't make you marry him."

I kept my face down, but inside I was smiling. All I had to do was hate Sir William, and Father wouldn't make me marry him.

'But what if you don't hate him?' a small voice inside me said.

'It doesn't matter,' I thought. 'I *will* hate him, I *will*!'

'Father thinks you'll like him,' the small voice inside me said. 'And Father knows you very well.'

'So what?' I thought angrily. 'I'll tell Father I hate him anyway.'

But that wouldn't work. I couldn't lie to Father. He could always tell.

If I liked Sir William – even just a little bit – I was doomed.

That morning, at lessons, Father Henry and I sat by the fire in the parlour and worked on my Latin. I couldn't make sense of any of the words. My head was too full.

What would Sir William be like?

Would he be horribly old?

Would he be ugly?

Would he be cruel? Oh, please God, if I have to marry him, make him be kind.

"Elinor," said Father Henry. "Are you listening to me?"

"No, sir," I said. He sighed.

"It will be all right, Elinor," he said, but I didn't believe him.

At supper time, I went up to my room. Alice combed my hair and helped me into my best silk dress. It was long, and dark red, with small pearls sewn around the neck. She rubbed sheep's fat into my face, to make it whiter. She reddened my cheeks. I wore the silver necklace that used to belong to my mother. What would she say if she was here?

"You look lovely, Elinor," Alice said.

But when I looked at myself in the looking-glass, I saw a little girl. A scared little girl.

In the yard, I could hear horses, and men's voices. They were here. I heard my father's voice and someone laughing. I felt like a wild falcon, trapped by a falconer, kept in the dark.

"Alice – " I said.

Alice kissed me.

"Time to go," she said.

The great hall was dark. The fire was burning in the middle of the room. The candles were lit. The smoke from the fire floated below the rafters, reflecting the light from the candles. The knights in the pictures on the wall waved their swords and rode their horses. None of them could help me.

The soldiers and servants sat at two long tables on either side of the fire. Father and Dan and Father Henry sat at the high table, with a man I didn't know. His hair was white, and his skin was grey and lined. He must have been nearly fifty. He stood up as we came into the room, and so did Father.

"Sir William," he said. "This is my daughter, Elinor. Elinor, this is Sir William."

"Delighted to meet you," said Sir William. He bowed. He had a strong North Country accent.

"Delighted to meet you too," I said.

I sat down next to him. I could see Dan, at the other end of the table. His face was red.

"This must be very strange for you," said Sir William. I nodded.

"Yes, sir," I said.

"It's a little strange for me too," Sir William said. "I have a daughter your age. You're younger than my son."

I didn't answer.

"Come," said my nearly-husband. "Don't be shy. Tell me about yourself."

"I don't know what to tell you, sir," I said, looking down. 'I wish you were dead,' was all I could think of to say.

"Well," said Sir William. "What do you like to do? Do you like to ride?"

"Yes," I said. "And hunt."

"Good," said Sir William. "You'll be able to hunt at my castle. And ride. What else? Your father says you play the harp?"

"Yes," I said. "Very badly."

Sir William laughed. "I shall hear you play very badly once," he said. "And then never again. What else do you like to do? Do you play dice?"

"Yes sir," I said. "And chess."

"Oh, chess." Sir William smiled. "My children like chess. We must play together sometime."

"Of course." I bowed my head.

"The castle where you'll live is right on the edge of England," said Sir William. "It's by the sea, nearly in Scotland. You can ride along the beach, and hunt in the forests. There are several other families nearby, with girls your age. It must get very lonely, living here with your father."

"I don't mind," I said, but what he'd said interested me. I'd never seen the sea before. I'd never had friends my own age – apart from Dan. Then I remembered that I was supposed to hate Sir William, and I looked down.

"Elinor," Sir William said. "I know this is hard for you. I do understand. But I think you'll be happy as my wife. I hope so."

"Thank you, sir," I said, very politely. I didn't look up.

When supper was over, we all got up to go and sit in the parlour. Father and I walked up the stairs together.

ııİİıı

"Well?" said Father, quietly.

I didn't answer. I wanted to tell him that I hated Sir William, but I couldn't. I knew he wouldn't believe me.

I didn't hate him.

I didn't want to marry him. I really, really, really didn't want to marry him.

But it looked like I had no choice.

Chapter 7
A Kiss

We sat in the parlour all evening. I had to play the harp, and sing. Father and Sir William talked about the war in Scotland, and Sir William said nice things about my sewing. Everyone agreed I looked lovely, and then ignored me.

All the time, I was looking at Dan and thinking, 'I wish I could talk to you.' And Dan was looking at me and thinking the same thing. 'We have to talk about this.'

I could think of one way to see Dan, but it was dangerous. If Father found out, I didn't know what he would do.

He'd probably send Dan away.

And send me off to be a nun.

If Sir William found out that we were meeting alone, he wouldn't want to marry me.

And no one else would either.

But I had to see Dan. I had to talk to him. No one else understood how I felt. And if I married Sir William, I might not see Dan again for years. Maybe never.

That night, I lay awake in bed and waited until I was sure Alice was asleep. Then I got up, carefully, trying not to wake her. It was dark, and I didn't dare light a candle. I didn't even get dressed – I put on my boots, and pulled my woollen cloak on over my slip.

I tip-toed out of our room, and into the corridor. Night was my best chance of seeing Dan. But Dan slept upstairs, in a big room with other men, Father's servants. I couldn't see how I was going to get in there without waking one of them up.

It didn't matter. I had to try.

I walked – slowly, slowly, oh so slowly – up to his bedroom door. I turned the handle and pushed it open, very gently.

The room was dark. Someone was snoring. Someone else moved, and I shut the door quickly.

It was too dangerous.

I couldn't do it.

I had to do it.

I pushed the door open again.

Someone was awake in the room. I could see a black person-shaped shadow coming towards me.

I shut the door. Whoever it was would see me if I ran, and there was nowhere to hide. I pressed myself back against the wall. It was dark. Perhaps he wouldn't notice me, there in the shadows.

The door opened. A voice said, "Hello?"

It was Dan.

Dan! I couldn't believe it. I grabbed his arm and pulled him towards me.

"Dan!" I said. "It's me! Elinor!"

"Elinor!" His arms were around me, and we were kissing, and I felt like I was melting, like I was sinking into his skin.

This was what I'd wanted. This was what I'd needed. This was what I'd missed.

I might never, ever feel like this again.

We pulled apart.

"I love you," Dan whispered. "I love you so much."

"I love you too," I said. I said it over and over and over. I might never say it to anybody, ever again. "I love you, Dan. I love you, I love you."

We kissed. And again. And again.

"You aren't going to marry him, are you?" Dan said. "I'll *die* if you do."

"I don't know," I said. "I can't see a way out. If I was ever alone with him, I could talk to him, maybe. But there's always someone there."

"I *hate* him," said Dan. His voice was low and fierce. "I'll *kill* him if he takes you away."

"No, you won't," I said. What a stupid idea!

Dan wouldn't really do it. He was just playing at being an outlaw, like I was playing when I told Alice I was going to run away.

But it was too late for playing.

This was for real.

Sir William stayed with us for three days. Every morning, he sat beside me at breakfast. Every evening, we sat together in the parlour.

On the second day, Alice and I were coming upstairs after a ride, when I saw Sir William. He was writing a letter in the parlour. He smiled at me.

"Elinor! Where are you going?"

"Nowhere," I said. I looked down, like I always did when I talked to him. "I'm getting my books for my lesson."

"Come and sit with me," he said. He nodded at Alice, who went upstairs.

I came into the parlour and sat on the chair beside him. This was the second time I'd been

alone with a man in two days. Would Sir William
kiss me like Dan had? I wanted to giggle, but I
was also afraid. When we were married, he'd be
able to kiss me as much as he liked.

"Don't look so shy," he said. He *was* kind. "A
husband and wife should be friends. I thought
maybe you could read to me. Or play chess,
perhaps?"

And that's when I had my idea.

"Let's play chess," I said. "And if I win, you
give me a present."

Sir William looked surprised. Until now,
I'd been so quiet. He didn't expect me to start
asking for things.

"And what if you lose?" he said.

"If I lose," I said, "I'll give you a kiss."

Chapter 8
A Chess Player

I put the chessboard out on the table. It had belonged to my grandmother. The ivory pieces were smooth and worn.

"White or black?" asked Sir William.

"White," I said.

I loved chess. It was my favourite thing. Better than riding. Better than hunting. Better than music, or dancing, or singing, or books.

For the first time in weeks, I didn't feel stupid, or shy, or scared. I felt like myself.

I stopped worrying about Sir William, and I stopped worrying about Dan. I just thought about the game. How well would Sir William play? Could I beat him?

Sir William was good at chess. He was better than Alice, and better than Dan.

But he wasn't as good as I was.

He didn't make much effort, at first. But then he saw he was losing, and he got better.

"Check," I said.

That meant his king was in danger. If he moved it to the right, he'd escape. If he moved left, I could beat him.

Sir William was thinking.

"You're good at this," he said.

I didn't answer.

'Of course I am,' I thought.

Sir William picked up his king. He moved it left.

Yes!

Three more moves, and the game was over.

"Checkmate," I said.

I'd won!

Sir William was smiling, but he looked surprised.

"Well played!" he said. "How old are you? Fifteen?"

"Fourteen," I said.

"I see I'll have to be careful," he said. "You're a clever woman."

'But will you give me what I want?' I thought. I didn't say anything. I just waited.

"So, what would you like?" Sir William asked. "A new horse? All my gold?"

I bit my lip. Sir William was a good man. Everyone said so.

"Please," I said. "Please, sir, don't ask me to marry you. I'm too young. I'm too young to look after a house. I don't want to leave my father, not yet. Please, sir, please marry someone else."

"I see." Sir William was quiet for a moment. Then he said, "Elinor, you do understand how important it is for our families to be joined, don't you? This marriage will help to keep you safe."

"I know," I said. "But not yet, please. I know I'm asking a lot, sir, but please. Don't make me get married, not yet."

Sir William sighed.

"Let me think about it," he said. "And let me talk to your father. I don't want a wife who doesn't want me. But I can't make you any promises."

"I know," I said. My face was hot. I felt like a child again. A stupid, ungrateful child. "Thank you," I said. "Thank you, sir."

I didn't see Sir William all afternoon. Alice and I sat in the parlour and sewed. We had a lot of work to do. It seemed I needed a lot of new clothes, now I was going to be married. Slips, and hose, and handkerchiefs, and veils, and good woollen dresses for winter in the north.

At supper, Sir William sat by my father and didn't look at me. I talked to Father Henry about the weather.

After supper, Father called me. "Elinor, can I talk to you, please?"

We went into his writing room. 'This is it,' I thought. 'My last chance.'

'Please, God,' I prayed. 'Please, please. Please don't make me marry him.'

Father said, "I talked to Sir William this afternoon."

"Yes?"

"He thinks you're a clever young woman," said Father. "He liked you a lot. But he thinks you're too young to run a house."

My heart started to thump.

"He needs an older wife," said Father, "Who can look after his land while he's away."

Thank you, God!

"So I don't have to be married?" I asked.

"Slow down." Father smiled at me. "Sir William and I both very much want our families to be joined. This marriage isn't just about you. You know that."

Oh. Yes. That.

"Sir William would like you to be married to his son, Adam," said Father.

His son!

"Adam is sixteen," Father said. "He's a squire, like Dan. Soon he'll be a knight. I met him last year – he seems like a good lad. He's good-looking, too." Father smiled, but I couldn't smile back. I was too shocked. "I think you'll be very happy together," Father said.

"But ..." I said. "Dan."

"I'm sorry, Elinor," said Father. "But you and Dan will never marry. His father has other plans for him, like I have other plans for you."

I was quiet. This was a good thing Sir William had given me. He was a kind man. I ought to be happy.

"Sir William says," Father smiled a little, "that he thinks you'll like Adam. He's an excellent chess player."

Chapter 9
A Prize

Alice was waiting by the door when I came out.

"Well?" she said. "What did he say?"

I told her what had happened.

"You're a lucky girl," she said, when I'd finished.

"I don't feel lucky," I said. "I should. I know! But ... what about Dan? I love Dan. I wanted to marry him. I can't imagine marrying anyone else."

Alice shook her head.

"Elinor," she said. "No one gets everything they want. Give this boy a chance. Maybe you'll love him too."

"Maybe ..." I couldn't believe that I would.

"Try," said Alice. "He sounds nice. And handsome!"

"True." I smiled a little.

"Most people manage," said Alice. "You'll see."

Sir William left the next day. He was going to see his son, and then bring him back here so we could meet each other.

One month ago I was going to marry Dan.

One week ago I was going to marry Sir William.

Now I was going to marry Adam.

Who would it be next week?

Father sent Dan back home, to stay with his father and mother.

"Just for a visit," he said. "You can come back soon."

Dan and I said goodbye in the yard, with the rest of the family there watching.

"Goodbye," I said. "Dan – *Dan.* Goodbye."

Dan's face was red. Father was watching.

"Goodbye," he said, staring at the ground. He wouldn't look at me.

I couldn't bear it.

I had to bear it.

I'm still me! I wanted to say, but I didn't. I stood beside Father, watching him go. When he'd ridden out of sight, I ran upstairs, and cried and cried and cried.

Sir William and his son came the next day.

I was reading with Father Henry when they arrived. Alice knocked on the door.

"They're here," she said. "Your father wants you to come and meet them."

We went to my room. I changed into my green silk dress, and Alice combed my hair.

"All right?" said Alice.

"Yes," I said. I held her hand tight. "What will I do if I don't like him?"

"Don't worry about that now," said Alice.

We went downstairs. Father was in the parlour with Sir William. He looked up and smiled as we came in.

"And here's Elinor! Doesn't she look lovely?"

"Very lovely," said Sir William. "Elinor, this is my son, Adam."

I bobbed down, keeping my eyes low. Then I looked up.

Adam was tall, taller than Dan. He wore a green tunic and red hose. He had high leather boots and a sword at his belt. He was long and lanky, with big feet and big hands and a big mouth. He was smiling. He wasn't as handsome as Dan ... but he looked kind.

"I'm very pleased to meet you," he said, and he bowed. He had the same North Country accent that Sir William had. It made me feel calmer. If he spoke like his father, maybe he would be kind like him too.

I looked at him again. He was older than Dan. And he was carrying a falcon on his wrist.

"What a beautiful bird!" I said.

He smiled at me.

"She's three years old," he said. "Her name is Joanne. She's a merlin."

"I know," I said. "My bird is a merlin too."

"You hunt?" He looked surprised, and so pleased that I nearly laughed. "Is there good hunting here?"

"Very. Perhaps you can hunt with us this afternoon."

"I'd like that very much," said Adam.

I looked down at my hands. We were both quiet. I kept looking sideways at him out of the corner of my eye. The second time I did it, he caught my eye and laughed. I blushed.

"I'm sorry," he said. "I didn't mean to make you nervous. Isn't this an odd way to meet each other? I'm still getting used to the idea myself. My father only told me about you yesterday."

"Did he tell you why he wants us to be married?" I asked.

"Yes." Adam smiled. "He was very impressed with you. I hope you like me. What will you do to me if you don't?"

I smiled back at him.

"I haven't decided yet," I said. "You'd better be careful."

We smiled at each other. My heart started beating faster. 'He likes me,' I thought. 'I know he does. And – what's more – I think I like him too.'

That afternoon, we went hunting. Father, Sir William, Adam and I.

Adam was a better rider than Dan. He didn't know the forest so well, but he could ride as fast as I could. He was a good falconer too.

We caught a hare, and three herons.

"That was wonderful!" said Adam. Father laughed.

"You sound just like Elinor," he said.

When we went in to supper, Father sat me beside Adam. Adam talked to Father about his horse, his falcon, his plans. I could see that Father liked him.

I sat and listened and wondered what I was going to do. I loved Dan. I thought I'd probably always love him. I understood why Father wouldn't let us marry. But I hadn't forgiven him for it yet.

I looked across at Alice. She was sitting at the end of the table, talking to Red-Haired Harry. She blew him a kiss and all the soldiers cheered.

If I was Alice, I could choose my own husband. I wondered what that would be like. Exciting ... and frightening too.

I'd never be allowed to choose a husband for myself.

And I'd never be allowed to marry Dan.

So perhaps I should stop wishing for the impossible. Perhaps I should take the man I'd been given, and be thankful.

Chapter 10
Dancing

Things were changing.

"You're a young woman now," said Alice, as we sat sewing my new dresses.

"No, I'm not!" I said. "I'm just the same as I always was." But I knew it wasn't true. I was changing.

"You're growing up," said Alice, sadly.

Dan was growing up too. He was going back home to live with his father. Soon he would be made a knight.

"My father's going to Scotland, to fight for King Edward," he told me.

"Will you go too?" I asked.

He shrugged. "Maybe. What do you care?"

Dan was angry with me. Angry because I was going to marry Adam. Angry because I didn't fight harder. Angry because he thought I didn't love him any more.

I did love him. I did.

I just ...

I thought I might love Adam as well.

Just a little bit.

Adam was kind. He was gentle. He was clever – cleverer than Dan. He could speak Latin, and French, and English, and a little bit of Greek. He'd read books that even Father Henry hadn't heard of.

"There are shelves of books in our castle," he told me. "My mother loved to read. I'll show you my favourites, when you come to live with us."

Adam and I were going to be married in the spring, in three months' time. Adam and Sir William visited us often in the weeks before the wedding. We played chess in our parlour in the evenings. Adam was a better chess player than Dan. Sometimes he beat me and sometimes I beat him. With Father and Dan, I could always guess what they were going to do next, but with Adam, it was always a surprise.

It made the game a lot more interesting.

In a few months, I wouldn't be living in Hardford Castle any more. I couldn't quite believe it. I'd spent my whole life there.

"You'll like our castle," Adam said. "You will, I promise. You'll like my little sister Rose. She's so happy that you're coming to live with us! She keeps asking, 'What does Elinor like to eat? What room should I give Elinor to sleep in? Does she have her own horse, or should we buy one for her?'"

"I always wanted a sister," I said.

Adam and I were married in our castle chapel. Father Henry said the words.

Afterwards, we had a feast – chicken, and wild boar, and beef, and rabbit, and hare, and duck, and a whole roast swan. There was music, and dancing. Adam was a good dancer. So was Sir William. Sir William and I danced a long dance together.

"I never thanked you for giving me Adam," I said, and he smiled.

"No, my dear, thank you. My son has married a wise woman. He's very lucky. I think you'll be very happy together."

"So do I," I said, and I meant it.

When the dance was over, Sir William went to talk to my father. A new dance started. I stood and watched the dancers. Adam was dancing with Alice. Dan was standing by the door, looking out. My heart jumped. I hated to see him so unhappy.

I went and stood beside him. I wanted to touch him, but I didn't. I stood and looked out at the yard.

It was cold. The first stars were coming out.

"Hello," I said. Dan didn't say anything.

"I'm sorry," I said. "You know I'm sorry."

Dan shrugged.

"If I could have chosen ..." I said.

He shrugged again.

"I know," he said. "I don't care. I'll be in Scotland soon, anyway."

He did care. I knew he did.

"I'll miss you," I said.

"Don't say that too loud," said Dan. "Your husband might hear you."

I went red.

"It's not my fault, Dan," I said. "Please don't be angry with me."

"I'm not angry," said Dan, but he looked angry.

"Let's be friends at least," I said, and he shrugged.

"Friends," he said bitterly. "A few months ago, you loved me more than anyone else in the world. Now you want to be friends!"

"I still love you," I said. "Dan! I do!"

"If you say so," he said, and he turned away.

Inside the hall, the musicians were still playing. The dancers were dancing. Adam came and stood beside me.

"Happy?" he said.

"Yes," I said. Was I telling the truth? I wasn't sure.

"What were you talking to Dan about?" he asked.

"Nothing, really," I said. Adam raised his eyebrows. He didn't believe me.

"He's angry with me," I said. "He ... we ... we used to love each other. He didn't want me to marry you."

Adam looked a little less happy.

"Do you still love him?" he said.

"I don't know," I said. "No, I do know. I do love him. But … I'm married now. Dan and I – that's over. I want to be a good wife, and I think you and I could be happy together. And we can't be happy if I'm still wanting Dan, can we?"

"No," said Adam. He looked thoughtful. "I was in love once," he said.

"Oh yes?" I was surprised by how jealous I felt.

"Her name was Christine." He laughed. "She was the daughter of a farmer in our village. I used to watch her in church every Sunday. I never spoke to her."

I laughed too.

"We'll be all right together," I said. "Won't we?"

"We will," he said. "I promise."

"I promise too." I took his hand. "Shall we dance?"

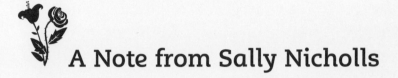 A Note from Sally Nicholls

The title, *A Lily, A Rose*, comes from a poem called *The Maiden's Song*. It was written in the 1500s. The poem is about a young girl who is going to be married. She stands with her wedding flowers in her mother's room, or bower, and listens to her wedding bells in the bailey, the tower. "How should I love and I so young?" she asks. She probably doesn't know her husband very well. And she might be very young; Queen Isabella was only seven when she was married.

A Lily, A Rose is set in the early 1300s. Upper-class girls had very little choice about who they married. They usually married young, to older men. Their husbands would be chosen for them by their fathers.

Some girls were happy with their new husbands, but others were not. In the play *Romeo and Juliet*, Juliet is horrified when her father chooses a man for her. In another play, *The Changeling*, Beatrice-Joanna is so unhappy that she pays to have her new husband killed. In real life, Christina of Markyate ran away from home and lived with a hermit in a wood rather than get married.

What would it be like to be fourteen and have to marry a man old enough to be your father? What could you do about it? *A Lily, A Rose* is my answer to those questions.

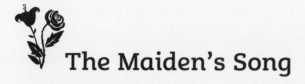

The Maiden's Song

When I was in my mother's bower,
I had all that I would.

The bailey beareth the bell away,
The lily, the rose, the rose I lay.

The silver is white, red is the gold,
The robes they lay in fold.

The bailey beareth the bell away,
The lily, the rose, the rose I lay.

And through the glass window shines the sun,
How should I love and I so young?

The bailey beareth the bell away,
The lily, the rose, the rose I lay,
The bailey beareth the bell away.

Timepiece Series

by Anne Perry

Troubled school girl Rosie Sands finds a series of very special watches which take her back in time. Rosie finds herself face-to-face with some of the most important women in history as they face their own darkest hours.

Will Rosie be inspired by their courage, or will the dangers of the past engulf her?

www.barringtonstoke.co.uk